Library of Congress Cataloging-in-Publication Data
Names: Schimel, Lawrence, author. | Lopes, Thiago, illustrator.
Title: Read a book with me / by Lawrence Schimel ; illustrated by Thiago Lopes.
Other titles: ¿Lees un libro conmigo? English
Description: English language edition. | Minneapolis, MN : Beaming Books,
    2020. | Audience: Ages 3-8. | Summary: Antonio wants someone to read his
    favorite book with him, but his mother and other adults in his
    neighborhood are all too busy except one, very unexpected new friend.
Identifiers: LCCN 2020005182 | ISBN 9781506465258 (hardcover)
Subjects: CYAC: Books and reading--Fiction. | Neighborhoods--Fiction. |
    Blind--Fiction.
Classification: LCC PZ7.S346297 Re 2020 | DDC [E]--dc23
LC record available at https://lccn.loc.gov/2020005182

VN0004589; 9781506465258; MAY2020

Beaming Books
510 Marquette Avenue
Minneapolis, MN 55402
Beamingbooks.com

READ A BOOK
WITH ME

by Lawrence Schimel

illustrated by
Thiago Lopes

beaming
books

MINNEAPOLIS

One bright morning, Antonio wanted to have an adventure.

He grabbed his favorite book.

But an adventure is more fun if it's shared, so he went in search of someone to read with him.

Antonio asked his mother:

"Will you read
a book with me?"

"I can't right now,
I'm busy," his mother said.
"But later tonight we'll
read together."

Antonio went down to the street.

He wanted to read his book now, not later.

He looked around for someone to read his favorite book with him.

Antonio entered the store beneath his apartment and asked the baker:

"Will you read a book with me?"

"I can't right now, I'm busy kneading bread," the baker said.

Antonio asked the woman at the fruit stand:

"Will you read a book with me?"

At that moment the mail carrier
was passing by and Antonio asked him:

"Will you read a book with me?"

"I can't right now, I've got these letters
to deliver," he replied.

Antonio saw the woman at the magazine stand.

With so many newspapers, she must love to read!

"Will you read a book with me?" Antonio asked her.

"I can't right now," she answered. "I have to put away these new magazines."

Antonio had tried at all the stores on his street.

"Everyone is too busy," he complained.

"Don't be sad, young boy," said a voice behind him.

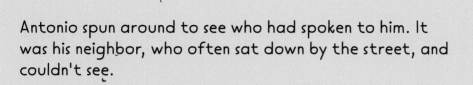

Antonio spun around to see who had spoken to him. It was his neighbor, who often sat down by the street, and couldn't see.

"How can you see me?" Antonio asked.

"I can't see you," the man replied, "but I can hear you. Come closer, I want to ask you something."

Antonio sat down beside him.

"What is it?" he asked.

"No one seems to have any time for me either,"
the blind man said. "Would you talk to me for
a while? Tell me a story."

A grin spread across Antonio's face.
He opened his book to the first page
and began to read.

Lawrence Schimel

Born in New York, Lawrence Schimel has lived in Madrid, Spain, for over 18 years. He writes in both Spanish and English and has published over 100 books in different genres. His children's books have been chosen for the White Ravens and by IBBY as Outstanding Books for Young Readers with Disabilities, among other honors.

Thiago Lopes

Early on, Thiago Lopes learned to communicate using images, and today he is an illustrator and graphic designer specializing in editorial design. He has illustrated several titles in Brazil and is a member of the Studio Kiwi, which develops, among other things, editorial projects in different languages, always combining illustration and graphic design.